Mary Had a Little Lamb

by
Sarah Josepha Hale

illustrated by
Laura Huliska-Beith

Marshall Cavendish Children

Marshall Cavendish Corporation

99 White Plains Road, Tarrytown, NY 10591

www.marshallcavendish.us/kids

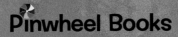

Pinwheel Books

For the newest Little Lee —L. H-B.

SCHOOL

Library of Congress Cataloging-in-Publication Data
Hale, Sarah Josepha Buell, 1788-1879.
  Mary had a little lamb / by Sarah Joseph Hale ;
illustrated by Laura Huliska-Beith. — 1st ed.
    p. cm.
  ISBN 978-0-7614-5824-1
  1. Lambs—Juvenile poetry. 2. Nursery rhymes,
American. 3. Children's poetry, American. I. Huliska-
Beith, Laura, 1964- II. Title.
  PS1774.H2M3 2011   811'.2—dc22   2010012807

The illustrations are rendered in acrylic, gouache,
and fabric collage on Strathmore board, and
assembled digitally.

Book design by Vera Soki
Editor: Nathalie Le Du

Printed in China (E)
First Marshall Cavendish Pinwheel Books edition, 2011
1 3 5 6 4 2

mc Marshall Cavendish
Children

Mary had a little lamb,

its fleece was white as snow.

And everywhere that Mary went
the lamb was sure to go.

He followed her to school one day—
that was against the rule.

It made the children laugh and play
to see a lamb at school.

And so the Teacher turned him out,

but still he lingered near,

and waited patiently about,
till Mary did appear.

And then he ran to her, and laid
his head upon her arm,
as if he said—"I'm not afraid—
you'll keep me from all harm."

"What makes the lamb love Mary so?"
the eager children cry.
"Oh, Mary loves the lamb, you know,"
the Teacher did reply.

"And you each gentle animal
in confidence may bind,

and make them follow at your call,
if you are always kind."

A Note about the Poem

Not everyone agrees that "**Mary Had a Little Lamb**" was written by Sarah Josepha Hale. Almost fifty years after the poem was first published in 1830, a woman named Mary Sawyer Tyler claimed that she was the "Mary" in the poem, and that the first twelve lines had been written by an acquaintance, John Roulstone, after he had learned that Tyler's lamb followed her to school in Sterling, Massachusetts. In 1825, Henry Ford, intrigued by Tyler's story, moved the schoolhouse from Sterling to Sudbury, Massachusetts, where it became a tourist attraction. Since Mary Sawyer Tyler never produced a copy of the Roulstone poem, most people believe that Sarah Josepha Hale is the correct author.